A
DOG'S
DAY

# I AM
# AVA,

## SEEKER IN
## THE SNOW

### Catherine Stier

#### illustrated by
#### Francesca Rosa

Albert Whitman & Company
Chicago, Illinois

To all the dogs and people who work together
to save others, and to Randy who braved the cold
to join me on a snowy adventure in Utah—CS

To all the rescue dogs and their owners,
thank you for your work.—FR

Library of Congress Cataloging-in-Publication data
is on file with the publisher.
Text copyright © 2020 by Catherine Stier
Illustrations copyright © 2020 by Albert Whitman & Company
Illustrations by Francesca Rosa
Hardcover edition first published in the United States of America
in 2020 by Albert Whitman & Company
Paperback edition first published in the United States of America
in 2020 by Albert Whitman & Company
ISBN 978-0-8075-1670-6 (paperback)
ISBN 978-0-8075-1669-0 (ebook)

Printed in the United States of America
10 9 8 7 6 5 4 3 2 1 LB 24 23 22 21 20

Design by Rick DeMonico

For more information about Albert Whitman & Company,
visit our website at www.albertwhitman.com.

# Contents

1. Up a Snowy Mountain. . . . . . . . . . . .1

2. Explosions. . . . . . . . . . . . . . . . . . 14

3. Becoming an Avy Dog . . . . . . . . . . 24

4. Saving Sophie . . . . . . . . . . . . . . . 34

5. The Demo . . . . . . . . . . . . . . . . . . .40

6. Star of the Show . . . . . . . . . . . . . 49

7. Star of the Snow . . . . . . . . . . . . . 55

8. Race Up the Mountain. . . . . . . . . . 62

9. Rescue! . . . . . . . . . . . . . . . . . . . .70

10. Among Friends. . . . . . . . . . . . . . . 77

About Avalanche Rescue Dogs . . . . . . . . 86

Acknowledgments . . . . . . . . . . . . . . . .90

## Chapter 1

# Up a Snowy Mountain

It is early morning and still dark outside. A light snow falls, but I'm toasty warm in the back seat of a comfy SUV. Ahead, I see the familiar gray outline of mountains.

Nate, my human best friend, is driving us to Osprey Mountain Ski Resort. I learned as a pup that a ski resort is a cool place where humans speed down snowy slopes while wearing long, skinny things on their feet.

But Nate and I aren't heading to the resort to have fun. We work there. We're a team. Nate is part of the resort's ski patrol. It's his job to keep the guests safe on the slopes.

And me? I'm an avalanche rescue dog, or avy dog for short. It's my job to find humans buried in the snow after an avalanche or a skiing accident. Many different dog breeds do this work, but Labradors like me—I'm a chocolate Lab—are some of the best at it. I'm three years old, and I've trained to be an avy dog practically my whole life! Nate says I can already hold my own with the best avy dogs on any mountain. But sometimes I wonder. We've never been called out to a real avalanche rescue—at least not yet.

Nate's SUV slows down next to a police car with flashing lights parked in the center lane.

We know the officer. It's our friend Carrie. She's stationed here whenever it snows.

Carrie checks to see that people have the right vehicles to drive safely up this snowy, steep road. If they don't, they'll need to turn around or put chains on their tires.

Carrie knows our vehicle checks out, but she waves at us to stop anyway. I know why. Nate opens the back window, and I lean my head out.

"Hey, Ava," Carrie says. "How are you doing, girl? How's the best avy dog ever?" She reaches over and scratches behind my ears. Carrie does this every time we drive by her.

"Have a good one, Carrie," Nate says from the front seat. "Keep 'em safe."

"You too!" Carrie calls as we pull away.

Nate drives up the mountain road into a

world of white. The flakes fall thicker as we go higher. Fresh snow blankets everything. It weighs down the branches of the fir trees. It dusts the jagged rocks along the roadside.

"Oh man, what a sight!" Nate says as we wind

up and up and up. "Takes your breath away, doesn't it, Ava?"

*Yep*, I think. And I wag my tail.

Here in the Utah mountains is one of Nate's favorite places. It's mine too.

We finally turn at a big sign into the Osprey Mountain Ski Resort. Nate parks his SUV and opens the back door. I hop onto the icy pavement. It's cold out, but my double coat of fur keeps me warm from the morning chill.

I lead Nate onto a cleared walkway through the snow. We pass a cluster of buildings. They're all frosted with white—the resort's restaurants and shops, the inn, and the ski lodge. We don't stop at any of them. Instead, we head to a plain building that houses the ski patrol station.

The ski patrol staff is gathering there for their morning meeting. They talk about the forecasted snowfall. They discuss trails that need to be checked, hazards that need marking. As their meeting winds down, I hear my name.

"So it's Ava's big day," says Javier, the ski patrol director. My ears perk up.

"Yep," says Nate. "She's going to be the star of the Avalanche Rescue Dog Demo today."

*I am? How cool! But what's a demo?* I

wonder. *Could this be my first real avalanche rescue? I've been training for so long!*

"Think she's ready?" Brandon, another patroller, asks.

"You bet," Nate says proudly.

Javier gives us a nod as we head toward the lockers. "Then we'll see you and Ava at the demo this afternoon at five o'clock sharp, right after the slopes close," he says.

After the meeting, Nate buckles on my

work uniform. The vest fits snuggly around my middle. Stitched across the side is a white cross, the symbol of the ski patrol.

Nate pulls his winter gear from the locker and suits up. His ski patrol jacket has a big, white cross on back that matches the one on my vest.

"Time to get to work, Ava," Nate says.

I know what comes next—and I can't wait!

We leave the building. Nate fastens his skis, and we head to the chairlift, a big contraption with moving metal, bench-like chairs. It brings people up to the mountain so they can ski back down. It's also how Nate and I get to our workstation—Ski Patrol Shack 1.

As we wait on the chairlift's loading area, I am alert. When the lift chair moves toward us, Nate gives a command: "Load up."

Nate sits down, and I jump on, front feet first.

The chair swings a bit, but I steady myself and pull my back legs up. No problem! I've done this before! I settle next to Nate for the ride. The slopes aren't open to skiers yet, so we're alone on the lift. Together, we glide past views of snowy firs and mountain peaks. I take in the smell of trees and snow and even the oily machine smell of the chairlift.

I wasn't always this chill about riding this swingy, open-air chair. The first time, when I was just a pup, I crawled into Nate's lap and whimpered. The ground looked so far away! What if I fell?

But Nate wrapped his arms around my shoulders and spoke comforting words. Soon, I saw the chairlift in a whole different light. How many working dogs get to start their day on a ride that soars through the sky?

Today, I feel soft flakes hitting my face. The breeze ruffles my fur.

*Oh man! I feel like a bird!*

When our chair reaches the top, we hop off,

and I run alongside Nate as he skis through the powder—the soft new snow. We head to the large log cabin that is Ski Patrol Shack 1. Nate takes off his skis.

Inside, it's bright and cozy. There is a kennel for me and the other dogs, with soft bedding inside where we can rest during the day.

For Nate and his fellow humans, there are computers and charts and maps. A big closet holds medical supplies. There's a coffeepot and a refrigerator. And there's that thing all humans seem to need—an indoor bathroom.

As Nate makes a pot of coffee, I shake melting snowflakes from my fur. Javier, Brandon, and a few other patrollers arrive.

It's just a typical, early morning in the snug ski shack.

Except…I keep wondering about that word

Javier used, *demo*. What's that all about?

I'm pacing around the shack when suddenly, a loud sound echoes through the mountains and rattles the windows.

*KABOOM!*

## Chapter 2

# Explosions

Nate's coffee mug clatters on the counter. Framed pictures sway on the wall. The *KABOOM* is followed by another sound—a deep, distant rumbling.

When I first visited the ski resort, I thought these *KABOOMs* were the sound of danger. Now I know better. It's the sound of our ski patrol's Avalanche Mitigation Team making the resort safer. The team's members are trained to use explosives. In the morning, they head out before the slopes open, looking for areas of heavy snow that might be unstable. Conditions like those could cause an avalanche—dangerous piles of snow and ice that rumble down a mountain.

Avalanches of all sizes happen naturally in these mountains, often after a big snowfall. But no one wants an avalanche to come crashing down when there are people below!

That's why our Avalanche Mitigation Team uses explosives to set off controlled avalanches instead, ones that collapse safely before anyone is on the slopes.

A couple more *KABOOMs* rattle the shack. Nate and the others don't even look up. They're already working, checking charts on a computer and gulping hot coffee.

The explosions don't bother me either. Some dogs jump at the pop of a firecracker. For avy dogs like me, loud noises are part of the job.

Another thing I've gotten used to? Here at the resort, I'm kind of treated like a celebrity. Guests wave when they spot me. After asking Nate if it's okay, kids stroke my fur and even grown-ups take selfies with me.

What's more, there's a framed picture of our resort's current and retired avy dogs hanging here in the ski patrol shack, and another in the ski lodge. We've been filmed by the news stations. There are even pictures of us on T-shirts and mugs in the gift shop!

Truth is, I'm not sure I deserve the attention and praise. Our other avy dogs, Flurry and Skate, have been here longer. They've done the tough work at real avalanche sites, outside the resort. Searches don't always end happily. Sometimes someone buried in the snow can't be rescued in time. That can be rough on both the dogs and their ski patrol partners. But Flurry and Skate still head out whenever they're called to do a search. They are the true hero dogs. Not me.

The door to the shack swings open. Flurry dashes in with Lorraine, his human partner.

Flurry is part golden retriever. Our other avy dog, Skate, is a Labrador with a shiny, black coat. Skate usually works out of Ski Shack 2, on a different mountaintop in the resort.

Flurry and I are good friends. I trot over to greet him, nose to nose. But not for long.

"C'mon, Ava," Nate calls. "You two can socialize later. Let's go make sure the slopes are safe."

Nothing makes me happier!

You see, I'm not only on call if there's an avalanche emergency. Sometimes I keep Nate company when he tackles other important jobs.

Nate picks up a backpack and goes outside to fasten his skis. I'm close behind. He heads toward a trail that is quiet now but often crowded with skiers when the slopes are open.

I sprint next to Nate as he skis to a large

evergreen tree. A safety barrier of orange netting
has fallen over. The orange netting is a danger
sign for skiers.

"Got a downed barrier around a tree well,"
Nate reports into his walkie-talkie.

I stay close to Nate, sniffing and exploring as

he fixes the barrier. Tree wells are dangerous for humans. A skier who gets too close to these holes in the snow that form under trees might tumble in headfirst. Making matters worse, loose snow could slide into the tree well, burying the unlucky skier.

We don't want that to happen to anyone at our resort.

Nate and I are nearly back to the ski patrol shack when we hear another *KABOOM*. It's far off, but in the distance we can see a ledge of snow where our Avalanche Mitigation Team has detonated more explosives.

First, a crack forms in the snow ledge. Then the white stuff collapses and pours like a giant bag of sugar tipped down the mountainside. Once this avalanche gets going, it kicks up big, fluffy clouds of snow as it cascades downward.

"Oh man," says Nate over the whoosh and rumble. "Isn't that something, Ava? Beautiful and terrifying."

I watch with my body tucked close to Nate.

Not every dog gets to see something this amazing unfold right before her eyes.

But as the snow crashes down the mountain, I am reminded again of the power and danger of an avalanche. That's why all the training Nate and I have done matters. If we're ever called for a search and rescue, we'll be ready.

## Chapter 3

# Becoming an Avy Dog

You may wonder how I got such a great job.

When I was still a pup cuddled up with my mom and brothers and sisters, Nate stopped by with Javier, his boss. Even then, Nate worked with the ski patrol. But Nate wanted to try something new. He wanted a dog, both as a ski patrol teammate at work and a pal at home.

As Nate sat on the floor with us pups, Javier gave him advice. "You want to find a puppy that is friendly with people and gets along with other dogs. A dog that's too dominant or too shy won't be cut out for this work."

Nate picked up one of my brothers. "Hey, buddy, nice to meet you," he said.

My brother whined and turned away. Nate set him gently back down.

"The best dog for this job is one that isn't too rowdy but still has lots of energy," Javier continued.

Nate leaned toward one of my sisters. "Hi there!" he said cheerily. My sister yawned.

"Most of all," said Javier, "an avalanche rescue dog has to have a strong drive to hunt. And an avy dog has to love to play tug-of-war."

Nate grabbed a pink piggy pillow and held it in front of me.

I couldn't resist! I hopped forward on my

little legs and chomped my puppy teeth into the fabric. Nate pulled, and I pulled right back. He pulled harder, and I snorted. I shook my head and pulled harder still.

Nate laughed. "I think we've found our avy dog!"

Nate visited a couple more times, until I was ready to leave my mama. Then he adopted me and brought me to his home. It was a warm, neat place with good food. Best of all, there was a blue beanbag chair that was the greatest place to curl up. I claimed it as *my* place.

At first, I had to learn human rules, like doing my business outside.

As I got older, Nate and I played lots of games. He would grab my favorite toy, a knotted cloth rope, and he'd shake it.

"Hey, Ava! Come on, puppy, puppy, puppy!"

he'd call. Then Nate would hide behind a chair. I'd find him, of course. I'd grab the toy he held out. He was strong, but I tugged and tugged till I got that toy!

Later, the games moved outside to the ski resort and got even better. Some of the ski patrollers would duck out of sight—but not just behind a tree or building. No, they'd actually hide under the snow. I'm not kidding! These humans would let themselves be buried in all that cold, white stuff.

Nate would give the command "Search!" Then it was my job to locate them with my nose and start to dig them out. Whenever I did, that human would bring out a toy, and we'd have a rip-roarin' tug-of-war.

I heard Nate call these games "training," but it seemed like playing to me!

One day, Nate loaded me, his skis, some gear, and a duffel bag into his SUV.

"Ready for your first day of avalanche rescue dog school?" he asked.

*Sure thing! I don't know what that is, but I'm up for an adventure!*

The two of us showed up at an unfamiliar building in the late afternoon. Nate had packed our stuff in that duffel bag, so I knew we'd be staying awhile.

At dinner that night, we met other humans and dogs from all over the world. There were new friends everywhere!

For the next four days, the trainers taught each human and dog pair to work as an avalanche rescue team. We played lots of

hide-and-seek games outside, finding humans or objects that smelled of humans. We even practiced an exciting nighttime search on a dark mountain.

"Ava has good instincts," one of the trainers told Nate that night. I learned that meant that I didn't run off after birds or squirrels while doing a search. But why would I? I can chase those critters at home. The hide-and-seek games on the mountain were much more interesting and challenging.

"So you think she'll make a good avy dog?" Nate asked.

"Ava is totally focused on the hunt. I think she'll be a champ," the trainer said.

I especially remember the last day of avalanche rescue school. The trainers brought us to a loud, smelly machine with whirling blades.

I was surprised when Nate led me to the noisy machine. Up close, it looked to be some kind of vehicle, with a big windshield. Nate lifted me inside first, then jumped in beside me. He gave the pilot a thumbs-up.

*You sure about this?* I thought.

I was even more startled when that machine rose right off the ground!

Nate held me and spoke soothing words close to my ear.

"Good girl, Ava! You're doing just fine on your first helicopter flight!"

I watched the ground fall farther and farther away. But I managed to stay calm.

When we landed, a trainer discussed how the helicopter ride was also a lesson. Since every minute counts during a rescue, avy dogs and their humans are sometimes rushed by helicopter to avalanche sites. A good avy dog needs to keep her cool, even in a loud, jostling flying machine.

I guess I did well at school. Soon after, I got my own ski patrol vest and began doing what I love best—working alongside Nate at this snowy resort.

Today, after checking the trails, Nate and I return to the ski shack. The day is bright now. Snow continues to fall. From the window, I see the first skiers clambering off the chairlift, eager for a downhill run on fresh powder.

All is well, so I curl up to rest.

I am just drifting off when a call comes in from the dispatcher. Javier responds, and his face clouds with concern. He turns to the patrollers gathered in the shack.

"We've got someone hurt on the slopes!"

## Chapter 4

# Saving Sophie

"It's an injury following a fall," Javier says. "A juvenile, eight years old, with a possible sprained ankle or worse, halfway down the mountain. Her dad's with her. The dispatcher says the girl's name is Sophie. Apparently she's a big fan of our avy dogs."

I perk up at the word *dogs*.

"Lorraine, Nate, why don't you handle this call," Javier says. "It's close by, over on Bluebird

Run. If Flurry and Ava are up for an outing, bring them along. They might be just the thing to cheer her up."

Lorraine and Flurry and Nate and I hurry outside. The humans grab an orange rescue toboggan from outside the shack. They put on their skis.

Soon we're all headed down the slope. Lorraine pulls the front of the toboggan, and Nate holds the long handles in back. Flurry and I dash alongside them.

Ahead, we see a girl in a blue jacket and ski pants sitting in the snow. A taller human stands close by. He holds the girl's skis and waves at us.

Nate and Lorraine swish to a stop beside them.

Nate unclips his skis and places them upright in the snow, crossing each other.

Lorraine does the same. The other skiers slow down as they pass by.

"Crossing skis so they form an X warns others that there's a hurt skier in this area," Nate tells the man.

The little girl is crying, but she brightens when she sees us dogs.

"We heard your name is Sophie, and you've had a fall," Lorraine says. "We're sorry your ankle hurts. But you're in for a treat today. We're from the ski patrol. This is Nate, and I'm Lorraine. First, we're going to check your ankle and settle you all comfy in this toboggan. Then you're going to *whoosh* along on the most amazing sledding trip ever to the medical clinic below. When you tell your friends about it, they'll all be jealous."

The girl nods, but she doesn't smile.

"Your dad will be close by, skiing right behind us," Nate says. "And you know who's going to be running down the hill next to you?"

"The dogs?" Sophie answers.

"Right," says Nate. "It will be like a parade down the mountainside in your honor."

At these words, the girl grins.

Lorraine and Nate ask the girl a few questions

about her injury. We dogs stay back while our human partners do their job. They fasten Sophie's skis and poles to the toboggan. Then Lorraine helps Sophie settle onto the toboggan and supports her ankle with a splint. Finally, Lorraine and Nate tuck a blanket around Sophie, then pull straps across the toboggan to keep her secure.

"Before we head down the mountain, would you like a quick visit with Ava and Flurry?" Nate asks.

The girl nods again, and our humans call us forward. From the rescue toboggan, Sophie smiles and pats us both. She turns toward my ear.

"Thank you for coming out and saving me," she whispers.

*Who, me?*

I am surprised.

My job is saving people. I know that.

I always thought that meant finding someone's scent and digging that human out of the snow. But Sophie seems to believe Flurry and I have helped her just by *being* here with her. That makes me wonder—can comforting someone count as part of a rescue too?

It's a thought I carry with me as the toboggan sets off and Flurry and I run alongside, kicking up powder with our paws all the way down the mountain.

## Chapter 5

# The Demo

Once Sophie is safely inside the medical clinic, Nate and I return to the ski shack. I'm ready to relax after that run!

The rest of the day passes quickly. Time flies when you're snoozing, I guess. By late afternoon, the chairlifts and trails close. It's time for Nate and me to return down the mountain. This time, Nate lifts me onto his back. What a great way to travel! I lie comfortably across his shoulders as he skis down to the base.

The day is still light, but a mist settles in. The lights on the buildings below twinkle through the haze. I remember what Javier said this morning—that this was my big day, and the demo would begin after the slopes close. I wonder what lies ahead for me.

On most days after work, Nate and I head to the ski patrol station. There, we get out of our gear and check out. Sometimes we'll stop at the busy ski lodge. Nate is a friendly guy. He likes to visit with the guests and the resort staff. Most evenings, there's a guitar player, strumming some of Nate's favorite songs. But I know what Nate likes best. It's those nachos that the lodge's snack bar serves! They're his weakness.

Today, though, Nate breaks routine. We don't head to the patrol station. We don't go to the lodge for nachos. Instead, we stop at a spot not far from the chairlift. Nate lowers me from his shoulders to the ground. He clips on my leash and snaps off his skis. We stand in the snow.

*What are we waiting for?* I wonder.

The clock tower's chimes ring out from the resort village.

*Bong! Bong! Bong! Bong! Bong!*

"That's our signal," Nate says. "It's almost showtime."

I tilt my head. *What does that mean?*

He leads me out a bit farther from the chairlift. We pass a sign stuck in the snow. On the sign, someone has drawn the ski patrol's white cross and a picture of a dog.

*Hey! Is that supposed to be me?*

Avy Dog Demo 5:00-5:30

RESCUE

Even though the slopes are closed, I see movement through the mist. People stream from the resort village toward the chairlift. But weirdly, no one is wearing skis. There are grown-ups, teenagers, and kids, all heading our way. Two youngsters in bright snowsuits are being pulled in sleds. A group of our fellow patrollers gathers by the sign in the snow. They greet the people as they arrive.

Javier jogs through the snow toward Nate and me and takes Nate's skis.

"You two ready for the demo?" Javier asks.

*There's that word again—demo. I guess this is it!*

"Sure thing," Nate says.

"Break a leg," Javier calls as we all head toward the crowd.

Nate laughs. "Don't worry, Ava. That's just

showbiz talk. It means good luck with your performance."

*Break a leg? I should hope not! And what performance?*

While Nate and I stand to the side, Javier sets Nate's skis aside and welcomes the crowd. "Thank you all for coming out today for this demonstration—the Ski Safety and Avalanche Rescue Dog Demo," he begins. The people look curious and interested as Javier speaks.

Javier talks first about avalanche safety, avoiding dangerous areas, and never skiing alone. Then he discusses safety devices that can help locate skiers. He describes something called an avalanche beacon that skiers in avalanche areas should carry and also special signal reflector strips that are often attached to ski clothing.

"But when someone gets trapped under snow without these, an avalanche rescue dog and handler team may be their best hope," Javier says. He motions with his hand toward Nate and me. The crowd looks our way. Nate waves. I'm not sure what I'm supposed to do, so I wag my tail.

"A dog's sense of smell is at least ten thousand times better than ours," Javier continues. "They can even identify the scent of a human under several feet of snow. Some

experts believe that after an avalanche, a trained avy dog can use that amazing nose to search a space as big as two football fields in just thirty minutes."

"That's incredible," I hear a woman say.

Javier nods. "And speed is important. If someone is rescued from under the snow within fifteen minutes and there are no serious injuries, the chance of survival is about ninety percent."

"So once the dog locates a human scent, she'll start to dig," Javier explains. "The handler will go to that spot in the snow and use an avalanche probe pole."

Javier holds up one of the poles. He shows the crowd how a patroller pushes the pointy-ended pole into different areas in the snow, trying to locate the victim.

"Once the probe hits upon something and it's determined where the victim is, the patroller uses a shovel to dig out that person as quickly as possible," Javier explains.

Then he says something that catches my ear.

"Now here's the demo you've been waiting for. Let's watch our avalanche rescue dog Ava and her handler Nate in action."

Javier turns to Nate and gives him a nod.

Nate leads me away from the crowd and says, "You got this, Ava. You know what to do. Just let those hunting instincts of your wolf ancestors kick in."

Nate unlatches my leash.

"You ready?" he asks.

Then he gives the command.

"Search!"

## Chapter 6
# Star of the Show

*Now I get it!*

A demo is another game of hide-and-seek. This time, though, it's played in front of all these people.

I shoot off in the opposite direction from the crowd. Even though my nose detects plenty of scents from that group—perfume, deodorant, food, skin, and other human smells—I know I'm supposed to find someone *under* the snow.

I run in the direction of the mountain slope. I detect a whiff of human scent as it wafts up from under the snow.

*Game on!*

It's hard to explain what happens next. All I know is that during this and every hide-and-seek session, it's the same. Suddenly, all thoughts in my brain and every muscle in my body click onto one goal—*must find that scent.*

Except it's a feeling so strong it's more

like one urgent idea pulsing inside of me:
*FindScent... FindScent... FindScent...*
*FindScent... FindScent.*

Honestly, the sun could turn blue. I'd never notice. I'm not focused on the crowd or the other sights around me. I hear only Nate's commands. I ignore all smells but the scent of human.

My excitement builds now as I can tell that I'm getting close.

*FindScent... FindScent... FindScent...*
*FindScent... FindScent*

Up ahead, there's a small mound in the snow. Could that be hiding the source of the smell? I streak toward it. The scent gets stronger and stronger as I draw near.

And then I'm at the mound. Now the scent rising from the snow is so powerful, I know I'm in the right place. I dive down, digging quickly with my paws. I use my muzzle to bat aside frozen chunks that cover a small opening in the hard-packed snow. From behind those chunks of white, I hear laughter. Nate catches up to me then.

"Did you find someone, girl? Huh? Who's in there, Ava?"

Nate helps roll away the snow chunks. I plunge my head in the opening in the mound. Inside, I see a glove, holding a rope toy.

I grab onto that rope toy and tug with all my might. I pull and pull.

The hand holding the toy is attached to a person in a ski patrol jacket. First a sleeve emerges from the snow, then a smiling face follows. With one more tug on the toy, I pull forward Brandon, Nate's friend and fellow patroller. Brandon wiggles out of a little snow

cave that kept him hidden. He kneels and continues the game of tug with me. He heaps on the praise too.

"Good dog, good Ava! You found me! What a good dog!" Brandon says in a cheerful, high voice.

I'm excited to play with Brandon, and I'm

happy for the moment. But I know this wasn't a real rescue. Brandon was never in danger. This demo was another training game.

I hear the distant crowd cheer. They clap their gloves and mittens together. One little boy pumps a fist in the air.

"Hear that, Ava?" Nate asks as Brandon stands and brushes himself off. "That's all for you. Let's go back and greet your adoring fans."

I feel a little let down—I haven't truly saved anyone. Still, I've made the crowd happy. More importantly, Nate is beaming with pride. I guess, for now, that's good enough for me.

## Chapter 7

# Star of the Snow

I see eager faces as Nate leads me to the group. Our audience stands, huddled together, knee-deep in snow.

As soon as Nate and I get close, they start with their questions.

"How old is she?" asks a little girl.

"Just turned three," Nate says.

"Where does she live?"

"She works here, but lives at home with me," says Nate.

"What does she do in the off-season, when there's no snow?" a young man asks.

"She gets time off. She gets to rest up and do doggy things. We go for walks, play fetch, even go to the dog park."

"Does she get cold?"

"Ava has a warm, double coat of fur to protect her from the cold and the sun. But people should always protect themselves by wearing warm jackets, helmets, gloves, and sunblock when they ski."

The kids kneel in the snow next to me, grinning as their parents snap photos.

One of the kids unzips his jacket for a moment. He points to his chest.

"See, Ava! I have your picture on my shirt!"

He's wearing an avy dog shirt from the gift shop.

*How cool is that?*

Then Javier makes an announcement. "We're going to close this area now, folks. But Ava here

and her handler, Nate, are heading to the ski lodge, if you want more pictures."

"So Ava gets top billing?" Nate jokes.

"Of course," says Javier, smiling. "She's the real star. You're just her sidekick."

Nate laughs. "I guess that's about right," he says.

"But seriously," says Javier. "Ava brings out the crowds so they'll listen to us talk about safety."

I hadn't thought of it that way.

On our way to the lodge, we pass some kids I recognize from the demo. They are in front of the inn, rolling big balls of snow.

"That was great, watching your dog find that guy in the snow!" a boy calls to Nate when we pass by.

"Thanks! And that's going to be an awesome

snowman," Nate calls back.

One of the kids giggles. "It's going to be a snow *dog*," she says. "Named Ava!"

"Even better!" Nate says, and the kids beam.

Inside the lodge, the mood is lively. Guitar music plays in the background. Nate and I move close to the big, stone fireplace. A fire crackles in the grate. A few people gather around.

"Can we pet her?" someone asks.

"Sure," says Nate. "Thanks for asking first. She's not working now, so it's okay. And she loves people."

I sit back and enjoy the pats, the kind words, and the gentle scratches behind my ear. It's nice and all, but I'm not sure I deserve the hero treatment.

Still, I've had quite a workout today. I'm already daydreaming about my favorite blue beanbag chair at home.

That's when Nate's walkie-talkie crackles with a message.

## Chapter 8
# Race Up the Mountain

Nate turns from the people by the fireplace to take the call. One little boy is asking me "Did you save anyone today, doggy?" so I can't hear what Nate is saying into the walkie-talkie.

Quickly, Nate turns back around. "Sorry, folks, got to go," he says. There's a strange catch in his voice.

Nate clips on my leash, and we run to the patrol station. He grabs a backpack and jumps onto a snowmobile parked there.

"Load up," Nate says.

We've practiced riding snowmobiles, so I know what to do.

I hop onto the seat in front of Nate. The machine roars to life. But then we do something out of the ordinary. We speed past the Osprey Mountain Ski Resort sign and leave the resort. We race up the mountain next to the road, then veer off to an area of backcountry.

I am all set for an adventure, a game. But Nate—well, with my back pressed against him, I can feel how quickly he is breathing. There's a particular smell coming off of Nate. It's familiar. Still, I've never sensed it so strongly before.

As we race through the trees, I remember the last time I noted this kind of smell from Nate. It was last winter. We had traveled together to an unfamiliar place. There were slopes and chairlifts, so I knew it was a ski resort. Just not *our* ski resort.

The patrollers with us that day held stopwatches and clipboards. Nate's actions told me that somehow, this game mattered more than usual.

Nate had given the command "Search," and I had streaked away.

It wasn't long before I found not one, but two people hiding in the snow in different places.

As I recall, no one else seemed as anxious as Nate that day. Not the other patrollers, standing with stopwatches and clipboards. Not even the two people who I sniffed out, hidden in their snow caves. All those people seemed happy and relaxed.

But not Nate. He was just, well, jumpy.

I thought that once I had found the two people that day, we were done. But Nate wanted me to keep going.

No problem!

It's what I love to do best. So I kept searching.

In short order, I found two objects hidden in different places at that resort—two human-scented shirts buried in the snow.

That's when a patroller holding a stopwatch gave a cheer.

"She did it! Ava passed the test! She located two humans and two objects in the snow in less than twenty minutes. She's an A-Level now!"

"Woo-hoo!" Nate yelled.

Nate came to hug me. His smell had changed. His nervousness seemed to have disappeared. Nate was Nate again—except extra happy and extra proud.

"Good girl, Ava. You aced the requirements. With an Avalanche Rescue A certification, we can work outside the resort. We can rescue someone in the backcountry too."

*Cool!*

I was happy that he was happy.

But tonight I sense Nate's nervousness, just like I did that day. Only more so.

Nate finally stops the snowmobile at a deserted, off-site area.

"Witness with a report of an out-of-bounds avalanche in the Kettle Ledge vicinity," Nate shouts into his walkie-talkie as he grabs his gear. "One person believed missing. I'm on-site, at the toe of the runout zone."

The scene is startling. A peak rises above us. Before us, there's a big expanse of white with bumpy boulders of snow. Clumps of dirt and gnarled tree branches poke up from the deep snow. It's just us—me and Nate out here at the edge of this avalanche debris field.

And then I get it.

*Maybe this isn't a drill or a practice.*

*Could this finally be the real thing?*

## Chapter 9

# Rescue!

Nate scans the area and continues to shout into the walkie-talkie. "I'm looking for signs of... Wait, I see something, a snowshoe, maybe. I'm sending the dog out."

First, Nate runs me a bit to one side, so the wind blows toward me. Then he kneels beside me.

"This is it, Ava," Nate says. "This is the most important hunt of your life. Now search!"

I take off.

An off-site hunt is different. There aren't many human smells here, like at the resort.

But as I run, the wind drifts my way. That wind carries just the tiniest hint of a smell that has risen up through the snow. My instincts overtake my mind and muscles. Only one thing matters.

*FindScent…FindScent…FindScent…FindScent… FindScent*

It's leading me away from the snowshoe. I run so fast that I overshoot the mark. The scent grows fainter. I turn quickly and head back.

Seconds count, I know.

I put my nose in the air, catch hold of the scent again.

It's different than most human scents I've found.

It reeks of distress.

This makes me run even faster.

I move my nose speedily along the snow to the place where the human scent is strongest.

And then I've found it—the right spot. I can sense it. The missing person is here, right here.

Frantically, I begin to dig.

The snow flies from under my paws. But reaching this human isn't easy. This is no shallow snow cave with a cheerful patroller hiding inside. This is someone in big trouble. I can smell it. I dig and dig and dig.

*FindScent...FindScent...FindScent...FindScent... FindScent*

Faster than I thought possible, Nate is by my side with an avalanche probe pole. While my paws scrape and claw to get to the trapped human, he plunges the pole into the snow—

once, twice. On the third try, he yells. "Hit something! Here! About three feet under."

Suddenly, there are other humans around—most in ski patrol jackets. I see Javier from our resort among them. They all have shovels and begin digging like their lives depend on it. All the humans are grim and serious and sweating.

Nate takes hold of the handle of my vest. "You've done your job, Ava. Time to let the ski patrol do theirs." My instincts tell me to keep digging, but I feel myself gently pulled back, away from the hole that's getting bigger and bigger.

Suddenly, the humans throw aside their shovels. They reach down and begin carefully lifting a man out of the snow.

"We got him!" Javier yells. "He's breathing."

While others tend to the man, Nate turns to me.

"Good girl, Ava," he says. There are tears in his eyes, but not sad tears. He pulls my toy from his jacket. "Good search, girl," he says as I bite down on the toy. It's the game we always play after hide-and-seek. This time, though, Nate's voice is different. It's filled with exhaustion and relief and pride too.

"Oh, Ava, you big, beautiful pup. Good dog! Good, good dog! You did it, girl. You saved a life."

Then he hugs me, and I feel Nate's whole body shaking.

## Chapter 10
# Among Friends

The next thing I know, the patrollers settle the man I helped find into a rescue toboggan. I smell and hear and see the helicopter coming in. It lands on the road not far from us. The man is brought through the snow to the helicopter and loaded onboard.

Nate and I motor back to the resort on the snowmobile. He parks the snowmobile, and we duck into the main patrol station. Nate sets down a bowl of fresh water for me. I lap it up, not realizing how thirsty I am till the first gulp.

Javier arrives at the patrol station a few moments later. He shakes Nate's hand. "You know I'm not one for fancy speeches, Nate," Javier says. "But you and Ava—well, that was one amazing search and rescue. You're both a credit to our ski patrol."

"Thanks," Nate says. "I'm awfully proud of Ava, that's for sure."

*I'm proud of you too, Nate!* I think, and my heart glows.

Then Nate unbuckles my working vest.

"Any news? About the man we found?" Nate asks.

"His name is Joseph," says Javier. "A witness saw him from a distance, snowshoeing by himself when the avalanche hit. Joseph is at the hospital now. That's all we know. We're waiting to hear more."

Nate nods. He takes off his ski patrol gear and stuffs it in a locker.

Then he puts on his own gray jacket and says goodbye to Javier.

"I'll keep you posted," Javier says. "I promise."

Nate and I walk back through the resort. It's mostly quiet, but for the wind rustling the trees. We pass the snowman—or snow *dog*—that we saw the kids making earlier. It's finished now, with pebbles for eyes and a pine cone nose.

Lights glow from the windows of the lodge. I'm ready to go home and plop into my favorite blue beanbag chair. But I think what happened tonight is so big that Nate may want to be among others. And Nate's friends will probably seek him out. I get it. Sometimes humans need humans.

Sure enough, inside the lodge, there's a circle of familiar faces gathered around a table. They greet Nate, and he goes to join them.

Carrie, the police officer we know, is with the group.

"I was just ending my shift when I heard about the rescue," she says to Nate. "That's incredible!"

"Yeah," Nate says. "It was…It was…"

He seems at a loss for words.

Carrie bends down to pet me. "Good girl,

Ava," she says. Then she adds in a whisper, "I always said you were the best avy dog ever, didn't I?"

"I had just made it home, but I turned around when I heard what happened," Lorraine says. "You two were so quick, the rescue was wrapped up by the time I got here. Great job!" Flurry is curled up by Lorraine's feet. He gets up and gives me a sniff.

Then Brandon pushes a big plate toward Nate. "Dude, we figured you'd stop in here.

Thought you might want to talk or hang out or whatever," Brandon says. "Also, we figured you'd be hungry. We ordered you your favorite—nachos."

Nate smiles and thanks his friend.

Still, I can sense that Nate is not quite himself.

I think about Sophie, the girl who injured her ankle today. When she was hurt and scared on the mountain, we dogs made her feel better just by being with her.

I figure an extra dose of good canine comfort from his best pal might help Nate too. I shuffle over to his chair. I push my nose into his palm and settle by his side.

Nate smooths back my ears.

I feel him growing calmer.

And honestly, I feel myself calming too.

Maybe Nate and I both need time for everything to sink in. I mean, what happened tonight—*it was a big deal.* Our work and practice and training all came together at a moment when it mattered most.

Then a new idea starts to dawn on me. Our rescue work can save lives—I get that. But I look back on the day and realize that maybe there's more to my job.

Javier says guests love to meet the avy dogs. When people come to see us, the ski patrollers have a chance to talk about staying safe on the slopes.

Then today, Flurry and I cheered up little Sophie. Even now, I think I'm helping Nate feel calm.

It's my job to be ready for an emergency. Yet even on an ordinary day, I help keep people safe and happy at the resort. I guess that maybe all along, I've been doing important work as an avy dog. I just didn't know it.

I look up at Nate. He smiles at me and rests his hand on my shoulder. I'm feeling pretty good about all we do as a team.

I know that eventually Nate and I will head home. We'll need to rest up for tomorrow. But tonight in the lodge, we're warm and sheltered. We're surrounded by friends. And we're together, Nate and me.

Right now, I know this is exactly where we should be.

At first glance, a dog's wriggling nose might not look like anything special, but inside, something amazing is going on. A dog's nose has about fifty times more smell receptors than a human's. That means their sense of smell is at least 10,000 times more powerful!

There are many ways working dogs use their superpowered noses to help humans, but one of the most important is through search and rescue. Dogs' noses are so sensitive they can smell tiny scent particles left behind by humans. This gives them the amazing ability to help find lost or missing people.

Some search-and-rescue dogs are called tracking, or trailing, dogs. These dogs are given a particular scent to pay attention to, and they follow it until they find the person they are looking for. Other dogs, like those trained for avalanche rescue, are air-scent searchers. Instead of following a particular scent, they look for "pools" of scent, or places with strong smells. This method is especially helpful when there is a lot of ground to cover, like in an avalanche zone. Avy dogs can search an area about the size of two football fields in half an hour. By comparison, it would take twenty humans with avalanche probes about four hours to search the same area! When just minutes can be the difference between life and death, it's no wonder why avalanche rescue dogs are the stars of the search-and-rescue show.

Besides having excellent noses, avy dogs need to have a strong drive to find what they're looking for. That makes breeds like Labrador retrievers, German shepherds, and golden retrievers great for the job.

Many avy dogs start obedience training when they are six months to a year old. After that, they begin rescue training, which takes a whole year (that's seven dog years)! While training takes a long time, for the dogs, it is a lot like a game. Handlers challenge their dogs to find scents buried in the snow, and when the dogs succeed, they get rewarded with play and praise. This type of practice helps the dogs become snow-sniffing experts, and when their training is complete, they are able to quickly locate people or objects six feet under the surface!

Once the dogs and handlers have completed their training and passed a test to become certified, they are ready to do the important work of responding to emergencies. And while no community wants to hear that there has been a dangerous avalanche, they can rest easy knowing they are in expert hands—and paws.

## Labrador Retriever

Labs were first bred to retrieve ducks from the water. Today, their hunting instincts make them great avy dogs, or at-home companions that love to play fetch.

**Height:** 21.5–24.5 inches
**Weight:** 55–80 pounds
**Life Span:** 10–12 years
**Coat:** Yellow, black, chocolate
**Known for:** Friendliness, intelligence, agility

## Golden Retriever

The golden retriever was first bred in the Scottish Highlands to be the perfect hunting dog for the rainy and rocky landscape. Today, these beautiful animals are excellent working dogs and wonderful companions.

**Height:** 21.5–24 inches
**Weight:** 55–75 pounds
**Life Span:** 10–12 years
**Coat:** Golden, cream
**Known for:** Kindness, reliability, confidence

Breed information based on American Kennel Club data.

# Acknowledgments

My thanks to Paige Pagnucco, avalanche education and outreach specialist with the Utah Avalanche Center, for graciously answering my questions and reviewing a draft of the manuscript. Thank you to Trevor John, avalanche dog program coordinator at Solitude Mountain Resort, Utah, who conducted the avalanche rescue dog demo I attended and kindly answered my follow-up questions. Thank you, too, to Sara Huey, communications manager at Solitude Mountain Resort, for her generous assistance in arranging my attendance at the live avalanche rescue dog demo, putting me in contact with sources, and for providing information and photographs of avalanche dogs at work. Finally, much admiration to the team at Albert Whitman, to editor Jonathan Westmark for his amazing insights, and to illustrator Francesca Rosa for the lovely scenes of Ava and her snowy workplace.

**Catherine Stier** is the author of several award-winning children's books and holds an MA in reading and literacy. Since it rarely snows in her Texas town, Stier traveled to a wintery ski resort to learn about and meet real avalanche rescue dogs. Despite their celebrity status, the avy dogs she met were quite humble and friendly—and of course, experts at their work! Stier grew up sledding and skating in Michigan, and now lives in sunny San Antonio, Texas.

**Francesca Rosa** was born in Italy and is a graduate of the International School of Comics in Milan. Since childhood, she has had an infinite love for animals, and they frequently appear in her illustrated books. Francesca now lives in the English countryside with one dog, Milù, and she hopes to add a corgi soon, as a source of inspiration and as a companion.